I0518778

MISHA ELLIOTT
PAISLEY WALKER

Copyright © Misha Elliott and Paisley Walker 2017

All rights reserved. No part of this publication may be reproduced, distributed, or transmitted in any form or by any means, or stored in a database or retrieval system, without the prior written permission of Paisley Walker and Misha Elliott, except as permitted under the U.S. Copyright Act of 1976.

This is a work of fiction. All characters, organizations, and events portrayed in this novel are either products of the author's imagination or are used fictitiously. Any resemblance to actual events, locales, or persons, living or dead, is entirely coincidental.

Thank you for downloading/purchasing this ebook. This ebook and its contents are the copyrighted property of the author, and may not be reproduced, copied, and distributed for commercial or non-commercial purposes. If you enjoyed this book, please encourage your friends to download/purchase their own copy. Thank you for your support.

This book contains mature content not suitable for those under the age of 18. Involves strong language and sexual situations. All parties portrayed in sexual situations are adults over the age of 18.

All characters are fictional. Any similarities are purely coincidental.

1st Edition Published: April 10, 2017
Editing by: Masque of the Red Pen
Cover Design by: 10dollarcover.com
Formatting by: Masque of the Red Pen

Blurb

Phoenix Dixon was the epitome of what you'd picture a rock god. With chiseled abs, bright blue eyes, and hair that would make any woman envious, he owned the stage for DIXON.

Hadley Anders was just a typical woman until the night she attended a DIXON concert. She'd always been a fan of the group, especially the lead singer Phoenix Dixon. She never expected that her life could change in the blink of an eye.

But what Dixon wants Dixon gets.

After sweating like a pig all night, it still amazed me that so many women would climb into bed with me. I wasn't complaining, though, because I was always ready for my dick to get wet. Especially after the high of performing during a sold-out show for thousands of people in New Orleans at the Superdome. I don't know what it is about being on stage, but I feel like I have the power... the energy almost emulsifies inside of me.

"Good job out there, Dixon," Greg yells out from the back of the stage, moving things around to get us ready to head out to Atlanta for tomorrow's performance.

"Thanks, man! We killed it, didn't we? Nick do what I asked?" Hitting his back, I walk by ready to peel these damn leather pants off my legs. I wish Candy would find a new look for me because these damn leather pants suck ass... especially mine. I feel like I'm a piece of meat in a vacuum-sealed freezer bag in these bitches.

"Yeah, man! Got you some weed and a couple girls to pick from waiting in the back of the bus. And let me tell you, that redhead is fucking hot, my man! Send her my way if you don't want her," he laughs as I roll my eyes. You never turn down pussy around here, even if it is an endless supply.

"You wish, buddy," chuckling as I walk toward my bus. The rest of the guys are still on the stage relishing in the crowd, but I prefer to get off the stage after being in the spotlight for the whole damn set.

"Just because I don't have killer hair and a sizzling smile, doesn't mean I can't get laid," Greg laughs as he picks up some more of the stuff in the back. "Okay, maybe it does."

"Never said you couldn't. See you tomorrow,

Greg." I shake my head as I make my way to the bus. I can hear the women in the back of the bus. Whoever I decide I don't want will end up going to the other guys, which they don't care anyway. *Most of them just want to say they were with someone famous, others think they can make us change for them. HA. I've never met a woman who could make me change my ways.*

Walking onto the bus, I smile when I notice all the chatter fade to silence. The women standing before me can't take their eyes off me, and their mouths are in the pristine position for my cock to slide between them. My eyes trail over the two blonde girls sitting close together wearing sparkly dresses and heels, which make me instantly think they are thinking about bagging a rock star for life. *I'll leave them for Carson.*

My eyes land on the banging redhead that Greg was telling me about, and man was he right. This woman's body is encased in leather, making sure you know exactly what's underneath that suit of skintight perfection. Her tits are huge and I'm sure store bought, but the bigger the better for me. Pointing at her, I smile. "Come on, pretty girl, it's your turn to rock my world."

The other girls whine, but she just stands, her eyes trailing over my sweaty body as she practically fucks me standing there. "Oh, I am sure I can rock your world, Dixon." Her tongue slides over her plump bottom lip.

"Good, then let's see just how hard you can rock me."

"Lead the way," she cajoles as she takes my hand, letting me know she wants exactly what I can give her... *A hard fuck and nothing more.*

Once we get into the bedroom, I don't give her a chance to speak before her lips are covered with mine. I make sure to kiss her enough to keep her bitchiness at bay, then I push her shoulders until she's kneeling before me. Her lips are pouty as she watches me slowly unzip my pants; grabbing those red locks of hers, I shove my cock deep into her waiting mouth. She doesn't disappoint me either, she takes every inch I give her and doesn't complain or push away when nine inches of meaty cock are deep in her throat.

"I'm not looking for love tonight, princess. But if you want a good raw pounding, stand up and let me bury this cock into that inviting pussy of yours."

Her eyes widen at my statement, and her body reacts. She's up and unzipping those tight ass leather pants and pulling them off. This isn't about being gentle, this is primal mating. I've got to be in Atlanta by tomorrow, so I can't have any stragglers on the bus an hour from now.

"Hold on tight to that wall now, sugar. I'm about to fuck you like you've never been fucked before." Grabbing a foil off the dresser, I bite it and quickly put it around my throbbing dick. *No way in hell am I getting in any woman without that thing on lockdown.*

"Mmmm, Dixon. Fuck me." Her voice comes out a throaty moan, and I can smell the arousal seeping out of her core.

Grabbing her curvy hips, I line up my cock with her soaking wet slit and slam my length deep into her. Repeating the motions several times before leaning forward and cupping her tits. She mewls as I pull her nipples over and over, sending her over the edge and taking me with her. Normally I wouldn't be so quick to fuck someone as hot as her, but I have places to be.

"Holy shit, that was amazing," she pants as I kiss her shoulder.

Smacking her ass, I smile when I hear her yelp. "Yeah, it was. As much as I don't want to see that sexy ass leave my bedroom, you're going to have to unless you're going to Atlanta."

"I knew the score when I got on this bus. I wasn't looking for forever, but I'm glad I got to experience a night with Phoenix Dixon."

"Was it everything you expected it to be?"

"Fuck yeah." She smiles as she stands, pulling the leather up her legs and buttoning her waist. She hands me a card, smiling. "If you're ever back in town and want a repeat, call me."

"Deal." I smirk as I read the card. Tawny, yeah the name matches her amazingly, and of course, she'd be a stripper with moves like she had.

"Night, Dixon."

Wrapping my fingers in that red hair of hers, I pull her lips to mine one more time. "Nice meeting you, Tawny."

I can't help but feel a twinge of pride when she falters on her own feet from my kiss. I used to be a decent guy, before women threw their panties at me when I opened my mouth, but I haven't been that way in ten years. Being on the road has hardened me. When you sell your soul to the Devil, you throw caution to the wind.

"You, too." She kisses my cheek before walking out the door, leaving me standing there watching as she goes.

I can hear the boys out there with the other girls, but I don't care. My itch has been scratched for the night, and I'm ready to get to bed. Another successful show and I'm ready for the next. Touring is starting to get old. I'm ready for this tour to be over so I can have some peace and quiet out on Papi's ranch. Collapsing on the bed—a place I never let a woman touch—my mind drifts off, thinking about music and other random things.

"What's up, Atlanta!" I can barely hear myself think over the roar of the crowd, but I love every second. The roaring in my ears keeps my adrenaline high as we play set after set. This is what keeps me moving on. "You guys ready to slow it down just a tad?"

When the confirmation comes from the rowdy crowd, I take my ass and plop it down on the edge of the stage. But what I wasn't expecting was a beautiful brunette woman with bright emerald green eyes to steal my breath from my body. I play the ballad that's about to release, my eyes never leaving the siren in front of me. If I could, I'd have grabbed her and pulled her up on the stage, but she was too far away into the crowd, and I couldn't get to her without being mauled to death by the other people wanting to touch me.

After the song is over, I stand slowly. Pointing at the woman in that Dixon band shirt and short cut-off shorts, I mouth, 'you're mine'. Those captivating green eyes widen as if she's a doe in headlights, but I mean what I say. *She will be mine tonight.*

I point to Jeff, making him come out on stage, yelling into his ear that I want her. He knows he better get her, because what I want... I usually get. And damn if I don't want this enchanting woman. I've never felt this type of connection with just a look, and I'll be damned if I'm going to let her get away without seeing what it's like to fuck her.

Hadley

Buzz Buzz The alarm on my phone chirps, reminding me that I need to get my ass in gear. Trish will be here shortly to pick me up for tonight. We are going to downtown Atlanta to the sold-out Dixon concert. Trish is lucky, her employer gives them some of the greatest gifts. Instead of asking anyone else, she insists on taking me for a special night out.

DIXON

I stare at the image of the woman in front of me, there is no outward sign of the broken heart or the days she spent crying. And there I go thinking about that asshole again.

My fingers sort through and remove several things before I can make up my mind on accessories. *Lipstick, where the hell did I put the lipstick?* After my breakup with Jack, I haven't been out of the house much. Well, not at all if I'm honest with myself, and that was the need for Trish's intervention. *Tonight is going to be full of fun and alcohol. You can do this. You're going to have fun tonight, and you aren't even going to think about what's his name.*

I'm finishing up my pep talk when suddenly there is a knock on the door.

"Come on, Hadley, you need to get your ass in gear or we're going to be late for Dixon," Trish yells again through the bathroom door. I still can't believe I agreed to go to this concert tonight.

"Dixon, Schmixon. They probably suck anyway." I open the door to find Trish on the other side, arms folded.

"How can you say that about your favorite band?" She gives me a *I'm not in the mood to put up with your shit* look.

"Easy, these days with all the equipment and whatnots live music generally sucks. Besides, I doubt they even sing live, they probably lip sync. Not too many are like Metallica." My words full of sarcasm, but Trish doesn't give up.

"Let me tell you, seeing Dixon live is going to be a religious experience. One we are going to miss because of your slow ass."

"I'm not slow, you came five minutes early. Besides, in order for me to wear these dangerously short shorts, I had to shave my legs. Since it has been a while, it took longer than I planned."

"What the hell are you wearing?" Trish's voice scolds me for wearing something she disapproves of.

DIXON

I look down, unsure what Trish is complaining about. I have on a pair of cute cutoff shorts paired with an old tattered tee of my favorite band, Metallica, and a pair of brown sandals. I'd say this looks great.

"Here, take that shirt off and put this on," Trish orders. She shoves a plastic bag from Spencer's in my hand. There's no telling what she bought from that place.

After removing it from the bag, I see it's a gray cotton tee with a photo of Phoenix Dixon on the front. He's wearing a leather jacket that's open, showing off every gloriously ripped inch of his massive chest. The name Dixon is in bright yellow letters that fall across his hips. *No, absolutely not. I'm not leaving the house wearing that.*

"Are you kidding me? How cliché going dressed like the ultimate groupie? What am I, seventeen?"

"Girl, you're killing me. You promised me one night of fun. So loosen up already," she says.

She's right, a promise is a promise. Besides, I'm not spending another Friday night on my couch binge watching Netflix. Trish has been there for me without question, and I don't want to ruin her plans.

Turning from her, I head down the hall to my bedroom to change my shirt and swap out my brown sandals for a pair of black strappy ones. When I emerge it's with a new attitude.

"I love the shirt. Thanks, Trish." She hands me my purse.

"Hello, Dixon, here we come," Trish shouts as we walk out the door.

Outside of my apartment sits a long black shiny limousine. Next to it stands our driver awaiting our arrival. Several other onlookers from the building come outside to take a look. A few passers-by turn around for a second look when they notice it's me.

"Good evening, ladies, you have a big night ahead of you." Our driver has a big smile on his face. He opens the door and helps us inside.

After he shuts the door, a giggle escapes my lips. We look around the space, admiring every inch. Trish finds the stocked bar, and she immediately pours each of us a drink.

When she hands mine to me, all I think is, *Oh my God I'm having drinks in the back of a limo.*

"This is going to be a great night, Hadley, just you wait and see. Cheers." We put our glasses together before downing our shots. "Do you want another?" Trish grins at me, and I accept. She pours us each another hefty helping; after all, we're here to relax and enjoy the night.

It's already starting off perfect. We didn't have to navigate through the hectic rush traffic of Atlanta. A girl can get used to this life of just sitting back to relax and enjoy the ride.

About forty minutes later, we arrive outside the venue. After making our way through the security checkpoints, we each get a stamp on our hand then make our way down the hall to the entrance.

Inside I immediately feel out of place, a mix of barely legal teens and twenty-ish girls wearing next to nothing mill about the space.

"You go ahead, Trish, I can stand back here for the show."

"Because this is the first night out we've had since the breakup, which means it needs to be as great as possible."

"I'm okay back here. Go on up front.

"Oh no you don't." Trish grabs my hand and literally pulls me to a spot just a couple rows shy of the front of the stage.

The moment he steps onto that stage I lose all self-control. His muscular arms move fast as he plays a shrill on the guitar. The flex of each muscle is so impressive.

Throughout the show he moves around; Dixon owns every fucking piece of the stage he steps on. I was wrong. This man is better in the flesh as the recordings don't do his music justice. My mouth drops open in awe as I realize I'm looking at a legend.

As he sings he grips the microphone tightly, then makes his way to the edge of the stage. Right in my point of view. I hate to admit it, but when he leans down as he sings in my direction I lose my shit.

Then he darts his tongue out of his mouth and up to lick his lips. He doesn't do it once or twice, he does it three times.

All I can do is think about all the things he could do to me. My panties are instantly wet as I think of the amazing tricks that tongue could do to so many places.

Dixon's voice lowers, and the houselights slowly come down to spotlight him in his moment.

Hearing him talk dirty is so invigorating. Yes, this is just part of the illusion of the show, but all I can do was imagine those sweet, delicious words are being spoken to me. Sweat glistens off those hard, chiseled abs, and all I want at this moment is to reach out and touch him.

My pussy is swollen and slick just imagining. Fuck, he's driving me insane. I know I've lost my mind because I swear his glorious finger points in my direction at the end of the song.

Did he just say what I think he did, to me?

"Do you want to meet Dixon?" I can't believe the man in front of us just asked if we want to meet Dixon.

"Fuck yeah, let's go, Hadley." Trish follows as the man moves toward the side of the stage.

"What? Trish, are you insane? We can't just go backstage."

"Uh yes we can, his guy was sent out here to get us." What the hell? I let Trish go in front as we make our way back over to where he stood.

"Hold on a second." The guy stops us at the edge of the steps. "Yep, if it seems too good to be true, it probably is," I inform her.

"The invite was only for her," he says, pointing a finger in my direction.

20

"What! I don't think so, I don't go anywhere without my friend, buddy." I turn to head back out into the main area and find the closest exit to get the hell out of here.

Before there is any distance between us, he reaches out to grab my shoulder. "Hold on there a second, let me double check. Don't go anywhere until I get back, alright?" As soon as he is out of sight I turn to Trish.

"C'mon, girl, let's go." This time I pull Trish to walk in toe with me.

"But didn't that guy say you were to wait?" she objected.

"I don't care, I'm not interested in going backstage without you, and besides, how rude is that to only invite one of us?

We fill in with the rest of the crowd and make our way outside to search for our driver.

"Wow, Hadley, you're a better friend than me. If I'm offered a trip backstage, you better believe I'd leave your ass in a heartbeat," she chuckles.

"Well, thankfully you didn't have to."

As we watch the driver pull up, two security guys dressed in black block our path. "Yes, I have her right here," one of the mystery men says.

"Okay, he wants you to get in and pull around to the back and wait," he informs us. Trish immediately gets in the backseat. After our driver is given instructions, we move around to the back entrance of the venue. There's a long line of female fans gathered around the Dixon tour bus. A thin yellow tape stopping them from getting too close.

What the hell is going on?

"What do you mean she LEFT?" I roar to Bart. The one job he had for the night was to make sure I had a pussy to bang, and when my eyes landed on that girl with my body clinging to hers in that shirt, I knew I had to have her.

"Well, well... you said her. I told her I didn't know about her friend and to wait there while I asked," he stutters.

I watch him for a minute, amused at the fact that a man so big and bulky could be so afraid of me in this moment. "Well hell, you should have let the friend come, too; one of the guys would love to fuck her brains out, too."

"I'm… I'm sorry, Phoenix. I just assumed you only wanted her."

"It's okay, Bart. I'm not mad, just find her, okay?" Placing my hand on his shoulder, I attempt to calm him down. He does a damn good job at keeping me safe, but unlike the other guys, he's way harder on himself than he should be.

"O. O. Okay," he stutters as he moves away from my grasp to find the mystery woman.

"Damn, Dixon. I've never seen you like this over a random chick. You may be whipped before you've even gotten it in," Vincent laughs as he slaps me on the back. He's the only one of us who settled down when he met Gracie. I can't blame him, though; she's a good woman. If he wasn't so good at bass guitar, he'd probably have left us long ago.

"I'm not settling down anytime soon, Vince. She's just got legs for days that I can't wait to wrap around my head as I make her scream my name."

"Yeah, you do that. I'm catching a redeye home until next weeks show." He pats my back before

24

shaking his head. He begins to walk off toward the bus, but turns. "One hundred bucks says you're about to fall."

"Two thousand says I don't." My eyebrows go up, in an attempt to show that I'm inferior to this.

"Deal," he laughs. "I'm ready for a bonus anyway."

Walking toward the bus, I see a crowd full of women screaming *Dixon.* Shaking my head, I decide to stay back and away from the masses. "This is starting to get old," I mutter as I watch the people screaming.

"Maybe it's time to take a break from the old ball and chain of touring," Jackson's voice comes from beside me. I look over at my best friend and lead guitarist. His long blond hair is saturated in sweat, and it's sticking to his face and back.

"Nah, I love the chaos too much."

"Yeah, yeah. I could use a vacation." He mutters something I can't hear after that as he walks away.

"Mr. Dixon. We've got the mystery woman in the back of a limo around back. If you'd like, we can put you in there and take you to the hotel for the night?" One of the men on the detail comes into my view as a smile comes over my face at the words.

"Friend with her?"

"Yes, sir."

"Good, Jackson!" I run after him, knowing he's the one who needs to tame the friend, and he wouldn't object. I'd rather him over Carter, because Carter can be a dick most of the time.

"What is it now, Phoenix?"

"Want a girl?"

His eyes light up while a huge smile takes over his face. "What kind of girl?"

"Come on, let's go get em."

Walking over to the limo, I make sure I put a little more swagger in my step in case she's staring out the window looking at me. When the driver opens the door and I see her sitting there, brown hair curled

26

around her face and emerald eyes glaring my way with her arms crossed over my body on her chest, I have to will my dick to calm down. I haven't blown my load in my pants since I was fourteen, and I wasn't about to let a woman be the reason I did it today.

"Hi there, I'm Phoenix, mind if I join you ladies?"

"No, thanks." She sighs as her friend's answer offsets her own.

I use that to invite myself into the limousine. "I hope you ladies don't mind, but I invited my best friend, Jackson Reid, to join us."

"I don't mind at all," the friend with the short skirt says as she licks her lips. "I'm a huge fan of you both." She smiles as she nudges her friend. "This is Hadley. She's a little nervous to be meeting her favorite band in person."

"No, I am not. I'm not nervous at all. I'm perturbed because he doesn't want to meet me, he wants to fuck me."

Oh, she's snarky, I like that in a woman. "Sugar, if I didn't want to meet you, I wouldn't have sent my men after you when you dodged me like a bullet." Sitting beside her I smile. "I would be lying, though, if I said I didn't want to get between those long legs with my very talented tongue."

She shivers beside me, licking her lips. "Well, who said I wanted you between them? You seem used to getting what you want, Mr. Dixon. I'm here to tell you, you can't always get what you want."

Leaning into her, smelling her sweet scent of fresh apples and maybe a hint of coconut, I whisper, "I always get what I want."

Her bright green eyes go dark with lust as she looks me over, taking me in. "You're about to find out that you don't." The challenge in her eyes makes my cock jump in my pants. She thinks she's going to walk away without me getting my fill, but she's got another thing coming.

"Challenge accepted, Ms. Hadley." I smirk as I see Jackson and her friend already making out in the corner of the limo. "Looks like you'll be stuck with me for a while anyway."

"Great," she huffs. "Look, I like you well enough, Dixon. Trish brought me here so I could get over my ex, but I wasn't expecting you to be the reason I got over him."

"No? Well why don't I come show you what it's like to be a performer on a stage?"

"On the stage?" Her eyes go wide with excitement.

"Of course. You can come up and see what I go through. Minus the crowd, of course." I smile, knowing that I may have just made my wants come true. No way is she going to turn me down now.

"Okay."

"Good, let's go." Taking her hand, I can't help but feel the electricity go through my body at her touch. *That's a first, maybe it's just static.*

Leading her through the now empty corridor to backstage, I smile when her hand squeezes mine a little tighter as she follows closely behind me. "You ready to be a rock star, Hadley?"

"I'll never be a rock star, but I'd love to see the view from where you stand at night."

"Well, then. Let me not disappoint." Smiling, I pull the curtain back, letting her walk out before me. I've never wanted to show anyone this, until her. The funny thing was, she thought she had the upper hand. But little did she know, she was about to lick me like a lollipop. I was going to make sure of that, and it would be the best damn lollipop she'd ever fucking tasted.

Hadley

"What the hell, Trish!" Here we are in the back of our limo after it got hijacked by one of Dixon's guys, and it seems that I'm the only one concerned about what happens next. Trish looks up long enough from applying a fresh coat of lipstick to her lips.

"Relax, Hadley, we're about to meet Phoenix Dixon." She waves her hand dismissing me and goes back to touching up her makeup. "God, I should've made sure you were wearing lace under that outfit," Trish remarks with a wink.

"Well, I don't like this. Just because he's some rock star who's used to getting his way, doesn't give him the right to act like he's lord of the manor with us." *This is 2017, not the sixteenth century where women were ushered to someone's bed chamber.*

"Don't you mean you honey? He wants you and it looks like he's gonna get it." Trish cocked an eyebrow at me. Damn, she's right.

I roll my eyes at her in disgust. My arms are folded across my chest. I knew I shouldn't have changed into a Dixon tee.

"Yeah, he spotted you right away. Looks like this is going to be a great night for you after all."

"I'm not that easy, besides after he who shall not be named and I split, random hookups are the last thing on my mind."

She stuffs her mirror in her purse, then puts her hand on my leg. "Look, honey, I know it hurt the way things went down, but that was eight months ago." Trish holds up for fingers on each hand and wiggles them to emphasize the point. "You need to get back out there and get you some." Trish looks at me sharply.

I lean back into the cushions and sigh, frustrated. Yes, she's right, it had been a while since I had done the naked twister with anyone. Hell, it was two months prior to my break up that we had sex. A man going for two months without even hinting at sex from you is normally a warning sign for every woman but me.

"You're right, it has been a long dry spell for me, but you know I don't make the best decisions when it comes to men obviously." Secretly, I envy Trish. She has always been the fly by the seat of her pants kind of girl. For her, men come with no rules—just fun. It's been so easy for her, while I lead and follow with my heart.

DIXON

"Hadley, get over it already. So you fell for a guy who was good at pretending who he really was, and it hurt. I get it. You can't let that stop you from living and making decisions just because one time it didn't work out."

As Trish's words began to sink in, I remember how I felt after I broke up with Beck. It isn't so much that my heart aches for the person, Beck could jump off a bridge for all I cared. In such a short time I spun these ideas of what life with him would be like. We had so many things in common, and I just saw him as the perfect fit to my life.

"You're right, I need to get over it and move on, but not like this. You know he probably does this several times a night with groupies. I'll come up with a reason of why we can't stay."

"Better think quickly because here he comes, and it looks like he's brought a friend," Trish says, leaning in close to me to watch out the window.

How did all of that get me to where I am now, which is going inside alone with Dixon? Oh that's right. "I'd love to see the stage." Those words came from my lips, and now I'm regretting them.

Dixon leads me by the hand through the back door and up a few steps to the stage. I'm about to see what things look like through his eyes. He pulls the curtains back sharing with me a part of his world. It's amazing.

We walk out onto the large stage, and it is the most breathtaking thing I have ever seen. I squeeze his hand a little tighter out of sheer delight and awe. This place is huge. All those now empty seats were filled just earlier tonight. Most people didn't sit, they stood like Trish and I and got in as tight as they could to see him up close and personal.

"I could never do this, it would freak me out too much. You probably love having all those eyes on you every night. Groupies who would do anything to just have a minute of your time." My words are truthful, but also harsh. I'm not interested in the idea of being with another womanizer no matter how tall, ripped, and sexy he is. He's in the entertainment business, and I know that if I let him, he'd be happy to give me the full Dixon experience. Something about that predatory look he gives me is a thrill. It has nothing to do with him being a big time rock star, but because he's pure unadulterated man.

"Tonight was different, I began to sing my ballad and looked over right here." Dixon points to the area where Trish and I stood for the concert. "Those big green eyes stared into mine, and all I thought about was this." Dixon leans in to kiss me, and I pull back releasing our hands. Taking a step back my mind races on something, anything to say to slow down the beating of my heart.

"So, Dixon, tell me where you're headed next." I stop moving backward when my hands hit the wall behind me. He takes one slow, deliberate step after another with that cocky grin on his face. When he's close enough, he puts his hands on either side of me, caging me in.

"I don't know if you remember, but after I saw you with my body pressed up against yours in this tight little piece of cotton you're wearing, you were warned. I told you, Hadley, you are *mine*." Dixon leans his head in to touch mine, and he sweeps his gaze over every inch of my body.

"You. Are. Mine." Dixon pauses once more. His eyes on me as intently as mine are on his.

"Fuckin' kiss me, Hadley," he commands, and I obey. My eyes close as his nose brushes past mine, and I feel his breath on me just before our lips touch. I'm not coy and have been kissed many times, but not like this. Dixon kisses me with such an intensity. He pushes his tongue in hard and deep, plundering my mouth. Our tongues duel for control, and he sucks mine deep into his mouth letting me know he's the one in charge.

Dixon's strong hand moves down to my breast, squeezing it and teasing the nipple through the fabric. I moan, and my body betrays me as it jerks from sheer delight. As he presses himself up against me, I want more. Daftly, he slides his other hand down the front of my shorts.

DIXON

Each time I cry out in pleasure, Dixon changes things up pushing his finger harder, further touching those sweet spots that trigger another round of intense sensations. My hands rove over his hard back, feeling the rigid shape of each muscle as I make my way down to the hardest one of all. My walls clench and tighten with his manhood in my grip, knowing that I won't be satisfied until I have him inside me. When Dixon invited me to *come* on stage, never in a million years did I imagine something like this.

Dixon

3

"Holy fuckin' shit." My cock strains against the zipper of my jeans. Each of her sweet little moans drive me insane. I can't think straight with the way this woman is making me feel. I've never felt this type of connection to a woman. When her eyes hit mine earlier tonight, I knew I had to conquer her.

Her lips connect with mine as her hand wraps around my thick cock. Our tongues our dueling in an attempt for control, but I know I'm going to win. Her eyes go wide when I wrap my slim fingers around her neck. "I want you to get on your knees and wrap those candy apple lips around my cock."

"I'm not doing it because you want me to, I'm doing it because I want to." Her hooded eyes look into my own as she kneels in front of me, sliding her tongue over her bottom lip.

My head goes back as I watch her, her emerald eyes looking into my blue ones as her tongue lashes out, swiping the pre-cum building on the head of my cock. The throaty moan she's let out makes my cock jump in anticipation of her taking me inside her hot little fucking mouth. My hands rest against the wall as I watch the little vixen below me take my cock deep into her throat in one motion. "Fuck!"

The woman winks, making my cock jump. Shaking my head, I close my eyes; reveling in the feeling her hot, wet mouth is giving me. "That's really good, Hadley. Lick me like a lollipop, baby." Using my left hand, I wrap it into her long brown hair, loving the feel of the thick locks between my fingers. Her eyes meet mine as I grip her tighter, taking control of her hot little mouth as I work my hips in and out. "After you make me come in that hot little mouth of yours, Hadley… I'm going to fuck you so hard you won't know where your body ends and mine begins. I am going to own you after tonight."

Her eyes go wide as my hips thrust forward and backward as my ass clenches. There is nothing she can do but let me use her mouth to fuel my own desires. A woman like her is probably used to being treated delicately, but I've never met a woman who ever made me lose control the way she has. My hips continue to pummel her wanting mouth as she makes sloppy gagging sounds, and her nails bite into my thighs. I'm positive she isn't used to being used, but I don't give a fuck right now. "Fuck!!! Ahhhh! So fuckin' good!"

She pulls off me after my dick is completely depleted, looking up at me with those stunning eyes, almost as if a doe in headlights. "That was so fucking hot. I never thought I'd like something like that, but it was amazing," she says and licks her lips.

"I agree with that, now take off those little shorts that have been fucking teasing me all night and turn your ass to me." Her movements happen seconds after I tell her to remove her clothes, making me smile. *She's eager to please me.* "Good girl, now put your hands on that wall. No matter what happens, don't you dare take them off of that wall until I say so." She puts them on the wall, looking over her shoulder, waiting for me to move. "Good. Now, stick your ass out for me."

Kneeling behind her, I smile as she pokes her hips out, giving me the greatest view of that perfectly plump ass of hers. Even the Kardashians wish they had an ass that looked like this without paying for it. "This is fucking beautiful, Hadley. Tell me it's mine."

She shakes her head, looking back at me. "I'm not yours."

Growling, I take my right hand, rubbing it over her ass before smacking it hard. "You will be mine. After I slide my cock into you, you will be mine. Got that?" She actually glares at me, making me smile. She's refreshing. *I've always been handed whatever I wanted because most women wanted the persona of*

Dixon. This woman is my match because she's showing me she didn't care if I was rock god, Phoenix Dixon, or Joe Schmo from around the block.

Leaning in, I spread her ass with my hands. "Don't take those hands off that fucking wall, Hadley." My tongue darts out, tasting her sweet hole as her body jerks at the sensation. "So fucking sweet. Men search for this their whole lives, and here I am taking it from a goddess." Her sighs make me lose my control, devouring her little slit with my tongue, sliding it up and down before spreading her ass cheeks further and running my tongue over the rim of her ass, waiting for her reaction. *She doesn't disappoint.*

"What the fuck?" Her hands come off the wall, and she jerks away from me. "That is not okay, Dixon. I am NOT into that!"

Rolling my eyes, I grab her by the shoulders. "I didn't do anything but lick the fucking thing. Baby, that ass is phenomenal. It deserves some affection. I just had to taste."

"I'm so done." She reaches for her shorts, but I stop her.

"I told you, you weren't done. You. Are. Mine. You're done when I say I'm done."

"Don't you know there's a thing called sexual assault, Dixon? You're treading a thin line." Her eyes blaze with anger and desire in one. She pushes my chest, giving me exactly the fuel I need.

"You are so fucking hot when you get all worked up. I'll leave your ass alone for now, but I will have it one day. You'll be begging me for it too. Until then I won't touch it again. But I am going to fuck this pussy. So turn around and grab the fucking wall like I told you to." Her eyes light up as she sees the desire in mine. I want her more than I want anything else. Hell, I may want her more than I wanted to sign the deal with the Devil I made ten years ago.

"I won't be asking you to do that. And I won't be going near yours either. There are just places that should be forbidden on a body." Her body turns, her hands hitting the wall.

43

"I'll remember that then." I smirk, grabbing her hips. I lean into her, biting her ear. "You clean?"

Her head turns, her eyes burning into mine. "Yes."

"On birth control?"

"Yes."

"Thank fuck," I grumble as I slam into her soaking wet pussy. Claiming her body as my own, slamming my hips in and out. This isn't about love making, because neither one of us is in love. This is about getting something we both crave and getting it now. Slamming my hips into her, I know with every thrust inside of her that I'm fucked in more ways than one.

I don't even know her, but I trust her enough to know she's not lying. If she is, I'll just have a damn kid, because being inside of her without a condom is fucking heaven on earth. Wrapping my hand around her hip, I slide my hand over her clit, working it with my fingers as I push deep into her over and over, taking everything I want. "Come for me, Hadley."

She shivers as my breath reaches her ear, and she explodes, making my already throbbing cock tingle with my own orgasm as her tight little cunt milks me to completion right along with her.

"Dixon." I can barely catch my breath. My knees are ready to buckle underneath me. I lean into the wall desperate for something to hold onto, but there's nothing there.

"Hadley, we need to go back to my hotel," Dixon says as he tucks himself back into his leather pants. Suddenly, I'm embarrassed at my disheveled appearance. Trish is still in the limo with what's-his-name.

"Hadley, come on. The next time I'm buried balls deep inside of you I want it in a bed." I barely have a second to breathe and pull my shorts back on before Dixon is pressed up against me. My body is sandwiched between Dixon and the wall. He grabs

45

my chin and tilts my face so that I'm forced to look him in the eyes.

"We're not done. I plan to fuck you every way imaginable, desecrate and own that sweet cunt tonight. And before you give me some bullshit about how you don't think it's a good idea, I bet that pussy of yours would say something different if I slipped a finger inside of you." Dixon presses his body even closer to mine, if that's even possible. His hot breath is on my earlobe.

"I guarantee that sweet cunt would latch onto me and not let go." He grabs a handful of my hair and tilts my head, exposing my neck to him.

"So, let me you ask you again, we going to your place or mine."

A streak of fear tingles down my spine at his words. Something about him makes me lose all control.

"M-my place." My mouth stutters around the words. If Dixon is going to desecrate me, his words not mine, I'd feel more comfortable in my own surroundings.

"My ride's out back." Dixon takes my hand and walks with me off the stage, down the back hall, and through the rear door. Outside, the limo with Trish is gone. There is another car, a sleek black Expedition, waiting in its place.

"Where's Trish?" I eye Dixon speculatively. "Where'd he take her?"

Dixon laughs, "Nowhere she didn't want to go, I'm sure. Here, Hadley, give your girl a call; check up on her, and let her know you're with me. Then get off the phone. I plan to be buried again between those fuckin' long legs on the way there."

The driver opens the door, and I slide in first, Dixon getting in after me. I look around the car to search for my phone, and realize I don't have my bag, which means I don't have keys to my place either.

"Address," Dixon says sharply.

"I don't have my bag, it was in the other car. My phone and keys."

"Drive back to my hotel, Jackson," he orders. The driver puts up the privacy screen between us.

Dixon reaches in the pocket of his jacket and hands me his phone. "Give your girl a call. I can make sure Jackson gets your bag for you."

I take the phone and dial Trish's number.

"Hello, who's this?"

"Trish, it's me. I don't have my bag so Dixon let me use his phone. Where did you go?" There is no place for privacy here in the closed space.

"Make it quick, Hadley," Dixon commands.

I try to slide over slightly to the side so that I can whisper what I want to say to Trish.

"You fucked him, didn't you? I knew it. I figured it made no sense for us to keep waiting for you two to come back, so me and the drummer took the party back to my place. We stopped for beer."

"Well, I didn't think you were going to leave me, Trish. I don't have my keys, so I can't get into my house." Dixon is on me, unbuttoning my pants and sliding them down.

"Well, can you meet me—" Dixon swipes the phone out of my hands and disconnects the call.

"Took too long, and I told you that I planned to be between those legs on the way back. We've got time, so lean back and find something to hold onto." His voice drifts as he positions himself between my legs. He takes my right leg and drapes it over his shoulder. *Holy shit. No man has ever had their mouth on me the way Dixon did. We just finished having sex minutes earlier and now he's...*

"Fuck, you're so fuckin' good." He spreads my lips apart, swiping his tongue from bottom to top. My hips begin to grind on his face begging for more. He greedily licks and sucks my pussy like he is starving right now, and the only thing to satisfy that craving is me.

When I feel the orgasm build inside me almost to the point of no return, I bite my lip, trying to not cry out. Dixon stops moving. "What. The FUCK!" My eyes open and see his face fixed on mine.

"What's wrong, Dixon?"

"Don't you EVER fuckin' hold back from me. I don't care if I'm making you come with my cock, my fingers or tongue—You come for me. You give me those sweet as fuck moans of yours. They belong to me like your body belongs to me. You got me?"

I don't know if that's a rhetorical question or not. I'm in shock and also very very turned on at the same time. The dirty way he talks to me is exciting.

"You got me?" Dixon says again firmly.

I nod my head, unable to say anything more.

"Alright, don't let it happen again. Hasn't anyone ever told you, you always have to give the devil his due?"

There's a knock on the glass. Dixon rights himself and helps me pull up my shorts. "We're about ten minutes out from the hotel. I'll get some food in you, and then I'm going to spend the rest of the night and morning filling you up with some vitamin D." After I get myself together, Dixon pulls me so that I'm leaning against his chest. Everything about this night is like a dream.

I see the sign for the hotel. He's staying at the Ritz. Of course he is.

Security detail is waiting for us when we arrive. "Everything you asked for is in the room, sir. Have a good night."

He opens the door, and I'm blown away. Never in a million years would I be able to afford a presidential suite at this or any hotel. Not with my salary.

"I have to handle something, I'll be right back. Get naked."

Walking out of the room, I look at Vince, my main security man. "Close the doors over there and go spend some time with your wife. I'm going to be fine here, and I don't want you missing out on a little family time while we are close to home."

"Phoenix... I can't just leave you alone."

"Sure you can. You can do it with pay or without... because if you don't leave me alone with that fucking goddess in there, I will fire you. I want no one to hear the sounds she makes other than me, because well... she's mine." My eyes blaze at the words. I've never met a woman who made me want to stake a claim. I don't know what the fuck this woman has over me, but I like it.

He laughs a little. "You whipped, Dixon?"

"Fuck no."

"Yeah, you are. That woman will have a ring on her finger in a month. Guaranteed." He looks at me with that cocky fucking *I know it all* look, chuckling softly, "Nothing wrong with that, man. Valerie was that for me, and if wasn't for her, I'd probably be dead by now."

"Yeah, yeah. She isn't more than a really good fuck for me. I don't do commitments, and once I leave Georgia tomorrow, I'll be leaving her, too," I snarl, not really feeling the words myself, but I have to. When you become a persona to so many women, you're expected to stay that way. Phoenix Dixon never has done a relationship. He isn't that man, but damn if Hadley doesn't make me want to change to be that man.

"Oooookay then. Valerie will like that you've given me the night off. Enjoy your time, Mr. Dixon." He shakes his head before waving as he walks away.

Taking a deep breath, I open the door of my suite. I don't know why they always want to give me the fanciest fucking room in the hotel. I may be able to afford it but the king-size room is good for me. Walking into the living room of the space, I can't seem to find Hadley. She's probably exploring everything, because honestly, there's a lot to fucking look at. I used to be enamored by all of this crazy ass fancy shit, but I'd prefer something not so in your face now.

I try to look through her eyes... eyes I used to see things with before my body and voice shot my band to stardom. I see the lavish and luxurious carpet and couches, the pool table and the grand piano in the room. *Maybe I'll get her on top of both of those later.* My finger runs over the keys of the piano, and when the silence ends, I hear the sound of running water.

Smiling to myself, I follow the sound of water hitting the see through glass of the shower.

I stand against the doorjamb, watching as the water hits her body, sending water dripping between her breasts and down to her swollen pussy. Beaming with pride, I strip myself bare, thankful to be out of those fucking leather pants. My cock is already harder than steel as I open the door. "Can't believe you'd get naked without me."

"Oh!" Her whole body jolts as she whips around, facing me. "You scared me! I didn't hear you come in… I was just trying to get some of the sweat off me." The mascara and eye makeup she was wearing is running down her cheeks, and even like this I don't think I've met a woman more beautiful.

"Well, shower sex is the best."

"I wouldn't know." Her lips pout a bit before I attack them, my fingers holding her neck as I devour her sweet perfectly plump mouth.

The whimper that's pulled from her mouth makes a growl sound in my throat. She's mine. I'm going to own her body, and I'm going to love every fucking second. *Wait what? Love. I don't do that word.* "You're about to find out just how great it is. Wrap your hands around me neck, Hadley." She quickly does as she's told as my hands grab the curve of her ass, my cock brushing against both of our stomachs. Hard body meets soft curves as I lift her, slamming my cock deep into her wet channel. The water is flowing from the huge showerhead, running down over our bodies as I thrust inside.

Her mewls and moans turn to screams as my body slams against hers. Her eyes are on mine as her body detonates, her orgasm taking over her body as we continue to fuck. Turning the water off, she looks at me confused. "What are you doing?"

"I'm going to dry you off with my cock still buried inside you, so you don't get too cold when I lay you on that grand piano and slide my cock into you like I've never done with anyone else," I rumble into her ear, making her shiver.

56

Never faltering in my step with her in my arms, my cock still buried to the hilt inside of her warm, inviting body, she smiles. "How's that?"

"Slow and soft. I want to remember every inch of your body before the end of the night." Wrapping a towel around her, I put my hand on her ass again, loving the fact that we never disconnected. Another thing I've never done with a woman.

"I don't want this night to end," she sighs, her eyes showing the sadness I know she's feeling.

"Why is that?"

"Oh! Cold!" She shivers as her ass touches the cool surface of the piano. I don't move, waiting for her to answer the question. Biting her lip and running a finger down my chest, over my abs, and down to my v, she looks up at me. "Because in the morning you'll be gone, heading on to the next woman who catches your eye."

Withdrawing until just the head is inside her, my blue eyes meet her emerald ones. "What did I tell you earlier, Hadley?"

"Nothing?" She moves her hips, trying to get me inside her again.

You aren't the only one being tortured, baby. This is killing me to not be inside you balls deep. "You. Are. Mine. I've never fucked someone more than once. But I did that with you." I slide into her, my eyes still on her. "I've also never done anything but fucked a woman. But I'm I guess you'd call it, making love to you. Right fucking now."

Her gasp sends me over the edge, and I suppose it's finally clicked for her that I'm not pulling her chain or fucking around. I. Want. Her. And she will be mine to have, forever. No doubt about that because what Dixon wants… He gets.

I couldn't get over what Dixon said. *"You. Are. Mine. I've never fucked someone more than once. But I did that with you."* His eyes never left mine as he *continued to move into me. "I've also never done anything but fucked a woman. But I'm... I guess you'd call it, making love to you. Right fucking now."*

Sure, he said we were in unchartered territory. We just made love. Even with my ex, I can't honestly say that what we came anywhere close to making love. Dixon could have any woman he wanted in his bed. The way the women crowded around the tour bus, I knew what they were after. Just a moment with him would be enough because they were in it for the notoriety and fame.

A stray thought made me smile, and Dixon caught it. "What are you all smiles about, babe?"

"Just thinking about how lucky I am to be treated to that nice cock of yours."

"Oh, so you just think it's nice. Don't you know nice it's something you call a guy's dick when he doesn't have much of one? This here is grade A perfection," Dixon says as he grabs himself with his hand.

"Don't forget your promise of food on the way over here. I think the alcohol has been a bit much for the amount of food I've had today." He didn't have to say it, I knew we were both thinking about something quite filling that I could put in my mouth.

"Okay, what does my baby want? You can have anything you want on the menu, just tell them to bill it to the room."

The cell vibrated on the end table in front of the couch. Dixon ignored it, at first. He leaned over to look at the number on the screen then placed it up to his ear and said, "Hold on." He placed his hand over the receiver and gestured toward the menu. "I guess I need something, too. Whatever you pick order two."

He strode into the next room to take his call. I picked out two dinners from the selections and asked for them to be delivered to the presidential suite. Since I was finished my first inclination was to go look for Dixon to see how much playing around we could do while we waited for dinner.

DIXON

When I walked in I noted the scowl on Dixon's face. "Slow down, tell me exactly what happened. No, it's fine. I told you to call if you needed me. Okay, you know I do." Even though he didn't ask me to leave, something told me that Dixon needed his space.

A knock on the door pulled Dixon from his conversation. "Hang on I have to get the door," Dixon said and set the phone down. I strained my eyes to get a name of the caller. It was easy to tell from the endearing way he spoke to her that they were close.

Hello, stalker. You don't have any claim on this man. Just calm down.

"Where do you want me to put this, sir?" The porter nodded then followed Dixon through the main room and into a small, cozy dining area off to the side. A tablecloth was laid out, and the silver candelabras were lit. Two dome-covered plates were set so that Dixon and I would be facing each other while we ate.

Dixon signed the receipt and made his way to see the porter out of the room. I sat at the table, waiting in awkward silence for him to return. He still had another woman waiting on the phone.

All the nerves in my stomach tied themselves up into a ball of knots. There were obviously some mixed signals on my part. Maybe Dixon was just being flirty and giving me a line that he did all other women who kept his company on the road. But he said that I was different, so I needed to find out if I could believe it.

When Dixon came back, he pulled me into his arms and kissed me deeply. With that one kiss all my nerves were calmed and replaced with jolts of excitement.

"Sorry to keep you waiting, after that call it looks like you are going to have me all to yourself, or for at least the next four days if you want." He touched my cheek bringing my gaze up to his. The soft touch of his hand on my face set me on fire. My heart raced.

He angled his head in again, this kiss was even deeper than before.

"I hate to have all of this go to waste, but what do you say we finish what we've started and come back to eat *after.*"

"I can handle after."

Blissfully sated and slightly sore after round two of piano sex, Dixon and I headed to the dining area for a now cold dinner.

We ate in an uncomfortable silence. I knew that Dixon had to be running down from the intense show tonight. My insecurities wouldn't allow me to open my mouth for fear I'd end up putting my foot in it.

"So you never answered me, you going to keep me company the next four days or not."

"I don't know. I guess I could... Are you sure?"

"One thing I'm usually sure about is not to ask something I don't already know the answer to."

"I'd like to spend more time with you, Dixon… I'm just not sure about how you'll feel once the novelty wears off. Your life is full of excitement, but I'm pretty boring."

"I don't find a single piece of you boring. Call your girl and let her know that you're going to be with me a while longer."

"Are you sure?" I asked, and he gave me a concerned look.

"Yeah, I'm sure. Mel called and said the next gig in Kansas is delayed because of the weather. They got hit with a bad storm, so we need to wait it out. I figured we could wait it out together—on this table, the piano again, maybe the couches, and definitely the bed.

"Who's Mel? You seem pretty close."

"Mel's a lot of things to me and the band. She's our tour manager, agent, and my younger sister." He reached out a hand to reassure me. "Come here, baby." I did as he requested and slid onto his lap. "I told you no one's had me twice, and no one is going to have me as much as you will over the next few days. Now make your call and get that ass back into my bed."

There was something about being able to spend the next few days with Hadley that kept me excited. I was going to do something for her that I hadn't done for anyone. I was going to take her home. I'd never brought a girl around my family… we weren't always wealthy. Before my band made it famous, my poor momma worked three jobs just to keep all five of us kids fed. I was one of those poor boys from the wrong side of the tracks, but I had a great face and good talent, or so the scout said when he found Dixon in a small bar we played at when we were out of high school.

DIXON

Watching her sleeping peacefully in my bed after a night of fucking and love making, seemed right. I'd never been this man, but something about her made me want to be. I don't do commitment, but I'd never been connected or drawn to someone like I am with her. Her brown hair is a gloriously hot mess, splayed out over her pillow and her face, but she is still beautiful.

Her ass is the most spectacular ass I have ever laid eyes on, and I've seen a lot of them. They remind me of a perfect globe on each side, and the curve where ass meets leg is phenomenal. I decide to let her sleep, knowing that she's worn out. I grit my teeth as I stand, the desire for her evident as my cock bobs as I stand. "Down, boy," I mutter as I make my way into the shower.

Stepping into the shower and turning the water on, I can't help but wonder out loud, "What is she doing to me?"

The warm water instantly soothes my aching body from the activity of last night. Trying like hell not to work my fucking cock up more than it already is, I move the soap-covered rag over my body. "Fuck," I hiss as the material slides over my sensitive shaft. The head of my dick looks almost purple, as if he's been deprived for years instead of merely hours.

Wrapping my hands around my sensitive dick, my mind replays all the sex I've had with Hadley as I continue to stroke my shaft up and down. My hand squeezes my dick, but I can't help but compare it to Hadley's pussy. That tight, wet channel that grips my shaft like a glove. Resting my head on the cool tile walls, I pump my hand over my sensitive skin as the other grips my balls. My body shakes as the release rocks through my body, sending globs of orgasm down the drain.

On shaking legs, I dry myself off, check to make sure Hadley is still asleep, and throw on a pair of sweats before making my way to the piano. Lifting the protector off the keys, I slide my fingers over it. I couldn't tell you the last time I played one of these for this purpose. There's a song brewing inside of me that I need to get out.

My fingers move over the keys as if I'd played this melody for years. It's almost as if my heart knows the song. I work on that melody and think about the words I want to go with it. It isn't until she sits beside me and lay her head on my shoulder, wrapped in the sheet on the bed, that I realize this is for her. It's about her. She's the reason I'm doing this to begin with. She's all but infiltrated my heart and I'm not letting her go.

Letting my fingers fall off the keys, I smile. "Sleep good?"

"I did, someone wore me out so much that I had no choice but to succumb to my world of fantasies." She leans in and kisses my lips. "But I'll be honest. My life is much better than my dreams right now."

"Well, you're simply stunning in the morning." Leaning in, I place a soft kiss on her temple. *What the fuck is wrong with you, Phoenix? You've never been this type of man.*

"What are you playing? It's not something I've ever heard from you before." Her eyes shine with questions as I close the piano and smile.

"If I told you, I'd have to kill you... and I rather like spending my time with you." Kissing her again, I stand, stretching my body from the hour of leaning over the piano.

"Thank you for the amazing night. I don't expect anything else, I hope you realize that."

Wrapping my hands into her hair, pulling softly to make her look at me. "Stop talking. You don't expect a thing, but I expect everything from you. I don't want just a random hook up with you, Hadley. I want it all." My lips attack hers again, and for once the woman just goes with the fucking flow.

"Stop talking. You don't expect a thing, but I expect everything from you. I don't want just a random hook up with you, Hadley. I want it all."

Did he really just say that? What does this mean for the two of us? Is Dixon asking me to be his? I don't even know him. My mind races as my lips duel with his. Liquid fire is coursing through my veins as Dixon pummels my mouth with his own. I can taste the essence that is Dixon, a hint of cinnamon toothpaste and coffee. My senses are on overload as I continue to let him take control of me.

"Phoenix," a moan escapes me as he kisses down my neck to my collarbone, and the sheet that was being held by my hand drops to the floor when they reach for him.

"Hadley, I want more from you. I've never wanted more. But with you, I want it." His eyes, those piercing blue eyes, look into my eyes, and I am gone.

There is no way I can deny that we are drawn to one another.

"I want you. I want to be more, too."

"Good," he growls out as his hands take my ass, squeezing as he grabs me, lifting me up and into his arms effortlessly.

I love that about him, because that isn't something that most guys I've dated could do. I'm a big girl, but I'm not skinny either. I love my curves so it's nice to see a man who actually appreciates them, rather than someone who wants me to run miles in a gym and eat rabbit food on a daily basis. That's so not me.

Squeezing my ass into his hands, gripping them, and massaging as he walks us to the kitchen counter. "Hadley, I'm going to fuck you. I need to claim every inch of you. Right. Fucking. Now."

"Please!" I can't help the whimper that comes with my breathless answer. I need him as much as he needs me. I should be embarrassed at the fact that my pussy is dripping wet and coating my thighs, but I can't because the look in his eyes shows me that he loves the fact that I am swollen and wet for him. *Only him.*

"That is one fucking perfect pussy. A sweet Georgia peach if I've ever seen one." He winks, causing me to laugh a little before the tip of his cock is rubbing against the wetness of my 'peach'.

"Oh shit! Don't go easy on me, let me know how rough it can be with you."

His eyes blaze with desire and a look that could scare me if I didn't trust him. "You don't know what you're asking for."

"Yes, I do. Show me."

"You asked for it," he hisses as he slams into me hard. His eyes on mine, his hand wrapped in my hair, gripping me and making me look into his eyes. He works his hips into me over and over again a few times before pulling out, making my body shake from the force of him. My tits are swaying still as he smirks. "Turn over, Hadley. I'm making all of you mine."

I just nod. I've asked for him to show me how Dixon does things, and he's showing me. He grabs my hips as his cock lines up with my pussy from behind, and he slams into me, making me scream. He isn't relenting either because this is what I asked him to do. I can't say I don't love it either. I love knowing that he's not just fucking me. Even if I only met him last night, this is not fucking just to fuck. It's not meaningless.

"You're sure you want me to do it all?" His voice is hesitant which makes me a little nervous, but I'm not backing down now.

"Mhmmm."

I feel his fingers dipping into my wet pussy filled by his huge cock before I feel them rubbing against my ass. "Dixon!"

"You asked, Hadley. I won't hurt you, I promise. Just relax." He slams into me with his cock again, hitting my walls and sending me into orgasm.

Before I realize it, he's already got two fingers inside my ass, and it's heightening my senses. I didn't think I'd like that at all, but with him… it feels like fucking heaven. "More, Phoenix. I need more, please."

"You want this cock in your ass, baby?" His breath over my ears has me trembling.

Is that what I want? Is that the more I need? "I want to try it."

"Oh fuck me. You are naughty. Stay right fucking there, Hadley. Don't you dare move. You do and I am going to spank that fucking amazing ass."

I hear him moving throughout the suite, but I'm not sure what he's doing. "Baby, I want you to take this. It's brand new, so don't freak the fuck out on me." A vibrator shows up into my hand, and I look at it and him like he's insane. "It's for your clit. Just listen. Put this on your clit for me and relax. It's going to make you feel pleasure during the pain. I won't lie and say it's not going to hurt at first, but once I get inside you and you're comfortable, it will feel so fucking good."

Biting my lip, I look at him as if he's crazy. But I did ask for more. "Now, I'm a little scared."

"I'll be gentle. I got lube and this. If you don't like it, we will stop, and I'll fuck that pussy until I explode inside it." His eyes are alight with lust and desire, and I can't say no.

"Okay."

He nods as he stands behind me, rubbing my ass with his hand before smacking it and watching the cheek bounce like Jell-O. "Turn that on and put it on your clit, baby."

I do as he says, my sensitive clit jumping at the sensation before I feel his fingers back on my tight hole. There's something wet on me; I'm sure he's lubing my asshole up so he can slide that big dick inside it. *Don't think about how huge the man is before he penetrates your no no hole, Hadley.* I can feel the pressure as he pushes against me, stretching my asshole around the head, sending a hint of pain through me, but I breathe through it as he slowly lets off before repeating the motion.

"Stay relaxed, baby, it won't hurt but a second. Keep that fucking vibrator on your clit. If it hurts too bad, I'll stop." His voice is strained as if he's trying to control the urge to slam deep into me.

"Don't stop. I'm okay, just keep being easy."

His hand rubs up and down my back as the other holds his shaft, pushing the head into my ass. The pain rips through me but is gone in a second. "The hardest part is over, babe. You are so fucking tight. Squeezing me like a damn vice, Hadley." His words come through his teeth as if he's fighting to keep that control he's losing.

"O... okay," my voice trembles, but he continues to rub my back, soothing me until he reaches under and grabs my sensitive nipple and pulls. "Fuck!" Screaming, my body bucks from all the sensations rippling through me. I don't know when he did it, but he's deep inside me now and squirting more lube down the center of my ass crack to get us both more wet.

"Let me know when you're ready for me to fuck this beautiful ass. Once you get used to my size, I'm going to fuck you so good, Hadley."

"I'm ready," I pant. Now that I'm stretched and ready, I have no doubt that I will enjoy every moment of what he's about to do to me.

His hips rear back and slam into me, sending a new sensation completely through my body. I would never in a million years thought that I would enjoy the things he's doing to me, but damn if it didn't feel amazing. If this is a sin, I don't want to ever walk in the light again.

Taking Hadley home is something I want, but fear. I don't know what she'll think of my home. It isn't what most would expect of a millionaire, but it's something I did for my family. Pulling into the driveway of Harlow Acres is always a great thing for me. My mother is Harlow, and I had finally been able to give her the thing she wanted in life. Security. Security for her children and for herself, something she'd worked for and could never do for herself.

Harlow Acres has over sixty acres and each of us—mom, my siblings, and myself—have ten of them to ourselves. My house is the most modest because I'm never there. A beautiful Acadian style home that has a beautiful porch and pergola over the back porch.

We grew up around Pigeon Forge, in a place called Maryville, Tennessee. When we were looking for a permanent place and I'd found these sixty acres, I knew this would be our home.

Each of my siblings got a home of their choosing from me, and so did my mother. I wanted them all to want for nothing, because growing up we rarely had what we needed. I was positive that Mama would be glad to see a woman who was actually stuck to my side instead of tossed outside afterward. I just hope they get along, which I'm sure they will. She reminds me of my mama.

"Oh my god! This is beautiful!" Hadley's voice breaks me out of my thoughts as I pull up the crepe myrtle outlined driveway toward the house. "This is not what I expected from you to live in, Phoenix."

"I get that a lot," chuckling, I park my Camaro out front, letting her take in the house. "I'll show you where you'll be staying the next couple of days."

She follows me into the house which I don't lock because sometimes Mama or the rest of them need something. She looks around as I show her the kitchen which is dark gray like the rest of the house, but has white cabinets and a sparkling black countertop, something I really wanted because of the contrast. All the appliances are stainless steel and there's a black and white backsplash above the counters. Sadie, my youngest sister, cleans my house every week to make sure it stays in good condition for when I come home. I can hear someone in one of the back bedrooms so I assume it's her.

Grabbing Hadley's hand, I can't help but smile when that now familiar jolt of electricity comes through my skin. "Come on, I'll show you my bedroom."

"This is a beautiful house. I can't believe I'm here with you. I feel like I'm dreaming, and in a moment I'll wake up from it and you'll be gone."

Grabbing her hips, I slam her softly against the wall, my lips attacking hers. I bite down softly enough to make her whimper. Before pulling away, my eyes shine with mischief as I lean in and whisper,

"I'm sure the soreness of your whole body would suggest otherwise, Hadley."

"Um. I would usually tell someone to get a damn room, but I'm kind of in shock that my rock star brother has a woman in his house." Sadie's voice comes from behind us, and I can't help but laugh as Hadley jerks away from my touch and looks at my sister.

"I'm Hadley. It's nice to meet you." Her skin is a bright shade of red, and I instantly feel bad for making this her first impression. Sadie looks her up and down, taking in her fitted jeans that hug that ass I love perfectly to the Future Mrs. Dixon shirt I had one of the guys get. *Funny, she really may be the future for me.*

"A groupie? Really, Dix? I thought we taught you better than that," she hisses further, making Hadley blush.

"She's not a groupie. I got that shirt for her. So fuck off, Sadie," I growl, letting her know that she is not to talk to my woman that way.

She actually looks embarrassed when I call her out on her shit. My sister, the baby of the family, looks more like me than the others with her honey hair down to her waist and stunning blue eyes that are wide set in her face. She's wearing a Dixon t-shirt as well as a pair of shorts and her Converse shoes. Most people don't know that there is a five-year age difference between us because she looks so much like me. "I'm so sorry. I'm just not used to people coming here with him. I'm Sadie, the bitch of a little sister."

Hadley laughs softly as she hugs Sadie. She's always so open with her feelings, and it's something I love about her; another trait that is just like my mother. "I may be slightly embarrassed, but I can see why you would say that. While I love your brother's music, I'm not with him for that. He's much better in bed than on the stage."

Sadie's eyes go wide while a huge hearty laugh escapes my mouth, and Hadley looks as smug as that comeback was. "Ew! Gross! I do NOT need to hear about it. I have to read it from groupies enough!

Gross! Let me go clean something." Sadie turns to walk away, but then smiles. "You've got about five seconds before Mama walks through the door to see who this woman is. I'm not good at secret keeping."

"Fuck me," I hiss. I wanted to take her to Mama not have Mama surprise the hell out of us.

"Watch your language, son! I don't like that, and you know it." Mama's voice comes from the other end of the hall, and I see Hadley's eyes go wide.

Well, five seconds wasn't even enough. Here we go.

Hadley

His mama? Here? Now? I'm going to faint. I try like hell to lock my knees to make sure I don't go anywhere, but it's like Phoenix can feel my anxiety as he places his hand on my hip and tucks me into his side.

"Don't you get all protective over that woman. I ain't gonna hurt her," the woman says as I turn to look in her direction. I see brown eyes where I expected bright blue, and fiery red hair. This woman looks like a spitfire. She's beautiful even though you can tell she's had a hard life before now. What I love the most, though, is the woman's cowboy hat on top her head as if she isn't the mother of a rock star. "I'm Harlow Phillips, Phoenix's mother."

Stepping away from Phoenix, I walk right up to her, sticking my hand out and making eye contact with her. "I'm Hadley. It's nice to meet you."

She looks me over before she pulls me into a hug. "It's nice to meet you. He never brings women here, so if he's brought you, you're special."

"Mama!" Dixon hisses.

"Don't you Mama me, Phoenix. I brought you into this world, and Lord help me I'll take you back out. Tell me this girl here, Hadley, right? She ain't special?"

"She's something special, alright."

"Exactly. Now, Hadley, I already know he's gonna keep you to himself since he has to leave in two days, but I look forward to spending time with you while he's gone. I want to know the woman who put that smile on my baby's face." Her hands hold both my cheeks as she looks into my face, letting me know that she is completely genuine. I like her.

"I'd love that, but I'm leaving with him, but I do promise to come back."

"Good. We will catch up then. Sadie! Let's give these people some privacy." Harlow winks as she looks at him. "Good to see you happy, baby. And sober."

"God, Mama! Get out of my house! And lock the door would ya!" Dixon yells out as he grabs my hand walking toward the back of the house.

Harlow laughs as she walks out of the house, muttering something I can't understand. He smiles, shaking his head as we walk out back to the yard that contains a beautiful pool with rocks and a waterfall that seems like a beautiful and tranquil place to relax after the stress of his tours.

"This is beautiful," I mumble as my eyes take in all the land filled with beautiful trees and things out in the distance.

"Well, they're the only ones who should be bothering us. Zander is off in the Military, Ryder is in college at Alabama on a football scholarship, and Grace is in New York pursuing a modeling career." His arms wrap around me before he kisses me softly on the top of my head.

Looking up at him I can't help but smile. "Thank you for showing me this side of you, I like it."

"Good, because I hope you stay around for a long time. I think a part of me would disappear if you did."

"I'm not going anywhere, except back to my apartment and back to work." Smiling, I kiss him, effectively cutting off the conversation as he picks me up and carries me back to the bedroom. He throws me on the bed and shows me just how much I'm fucked when it comes to him. I'm whipped, and there isn't a damn thing that can keep me from going anywhere. I. Am. His.

"Bitch, you better get to spilling your guts! I haven't heard from you since you left me in that limo with Mr. Sex on a fucking stick." Trish smiles from my couch as she waits for the details.

"Trish, I don't know how to explain it. He is amazing, and I think I'm in love with him. He's amazing in bed, but he's great out of it. He loves his siblings and his mother. The man you all see is only the tip of the iceberg to him." I sigh, thinking about the past week I spent with Phoenix. It was amazing getting to know him. I don't know what set me apart from the rest of them, but I sure as hell am glad I have it.

"Speaking of your man, here he is on TMZ." Trish grabs the remote, turning the trash of a show on. *I hate TMZ, with a passion.*

"Seems like the lead star of Dixon, likes to play the field. Sources close to the star claim he found a new love interest, which isn't like Dixon at all. But he may just be back to his old ways." The blonde woman reporting makes me sick, but her words send me heart into my stomach.

"Phoenix Dixon was with a mystery woman since the concert in Georgia, but as soon as she was back home it looks like he went back to his playboy ways. Here's a picture of him with a blonde attached to his lips in what looks like a lover's embrace."

Trish quickly turns the T.V. off just as my phone starts ringing. His picture pops up on the screen, and I don't even think about what I'm doing. I lob that fucking thing straight at the T.V. where his head was. "I should have fucking known!" I sob as my legs give way.

Trish comes to stand by me and sighs. "I don't think they saw the whole story. You need to talk to him, Hadley. It could just be a huge misunderstanding."

"Or he could have just been a complete and total ass with a horrible desire to hurt someone!" I sob out, lashing at her. "You're the reason I ever met him! Just get out, please!"

"Hey! This isn't my fucking fault!" She yells out, but the look on my face lets her know that I am five seconds from taking it out on her. "Fine, but call me when you get a new damn phone. I didn't do that shit on purpose."

Once the door closes, I break down, falling into myself and just letting the emotions take over. It isn't until I'm finally asleep that I feel arms around me and the scent of the man I loath, fill my senses. Only then do I succumb to the numbness I have begged for. Funny how you can hate someone so much, but they are the thing that holds you together.

"Thank you, Los Angeles! You've been wonderful as always! Come back and see us when we visit again!" The crowd goes wild as we make our way off the stage after our encore. I can't wait to get back to the bus, so I can call Hadley and see what she's doing. I've been working on that song for her, and I hope she likes it. I've never been so emotionally cut open when I've written a song, but this one is cutting deep.

"Dude, that chick you hooked me up with, Trish... Bitch could suck a mean dick. Too bad she only wanted a hook up because I might have gotten whipped if she hadn't." Jackson slaps my back as we walk toward the bus.

"Dixon!" A woman's voice fills my ears just as a body flings into my arms, and lips hit mine. Two security guards pull her off me before I realize that there are cameras all around. Nothing I'm not used to, but all I can think about is what the hell Hadley will think if I don't tell her before she sees it.

"Come on, miss, you aren't allowed back here," Bart yells out as he pulls her toward the barrier.

"How the fuck did she get back here?" I hiss, looking at all the guys. They all shrug, unsure how she got in, but that's something I will find out. "Shit! Hadley is going to fucking freak."

"Damn, you are whipped." Jackson's head shakes as we get onto the bus. "I knew she was different, but I wasn't sure if she was different enough to cause you to go monogamous."

Throwing my sweaty leather jacket off, I grumble, "Dude, she's mine. I'm not interested in anyone else anymore. Especially not the woman who probably just fucked it up for me." Once I feel the cool air of the bus on my heated skin, I can't help but sigh. I've been blazing on the stage with those lights, but it pays the bills, and I enjoy singing my own songs. "I'm going to shower. If shit happens with that, let me know."

Once I get into my room, away from the women the guys brought for the others, I step under the spray of the showerhead. It's not like the ones in the hotels, but it does get the grime off me, and that woman's taste off my lips. The adrenaline pumping through me makes my cock rock hard, and the woman I spent a week balls deep inside comes to my mind. I really need to talk to her about coming on tour with me, because dammit, I'm tired of taking matters into my own hand when she isn't around.

"Wrap that up, Phoenix! Shit's happening!" Jackson's voice fills my ears as my hand wraps around my cock. *Well, fuck me.*

"Coming!" I yell, only I wish I was coming instead. After getting out of the shower, I wrap a towel around my waist and stalk out to the main cabin. The women who are waiting for the other guys are staring, but I don't give a fuck. I only care about one. "What the fuck is going on?" I hiss, making them jump. But again, I don't give a fuck.

"TMZ. You were on it. Kissing that bitch."

"FUCK!" Storming back into my room, my chest heaving, I call Hadley. It rings before going to voicemail. "FUCK!" My finger hits the redial button, only to go straight to voicemail again. This cycle repeats and repeats until I finally get fed up. Throwing a pair of jeans and a shirt on, I grab my wallet and Bert. "Get Mel on the fucking phone. Tell her I need a redeye to Georgia. NOW!"

He nods as we get into a car and head for the airport. She can ignore my calls for as long as she wants, but she won't ignore me banging on her door. He leaves me at the airport on the redeye to Atlanta. I know exactly where she is since I dropped her off, and I knew exactly where she keeps that spare key. I never thought I'd have to use it, but I know if she isn't answering my calls, that she wouldn't answer the door either.

94

DIXON

Standing on her doorstep, I'm nervous. While she doesn't think so, she has the power to shatter me. Break me, and that scares the shit out of me. *What if she turns me away without hearing the truth?*

Unlocking the door, my eyes land on the shattered television and iPhone sitting on the floor. *Well, I better watch my fucking balls tonight.* "Hadley?" Looking around the room, I see her feet curled in a ball behind the couch. My heart breaks seeing her that way and knowing that I was the reason behind it.

"Hadley?" Leaning down, I grab her, pulling her into my chest and looking at her for the first time. Her eyes are swollen and blotchy from the tears she's cried. Tears from me. "Baby, I am so sorry, but it isn't what you think."

She shakes her head, trying to push me away, but she doesn't have the strength. I walk her to her bedroom, cuddling her into my chest as I lay us both across the bed and pull her into me. She may hate me tomorrow, but for tonight she's using me as her strength, and I will relish it for a little longer.

Dixon calls my name, but I'm unable to respond. Maybe it's shock. After everything that has happened, the last thing I imagined was him coming to see me. Being curled up next to him feels like a dream. I'm unable to move; we're void of any expression, like statues staring at one another. My heart stops beating; my lungs are exhausted of air.

It's like I'm sleepwalking through someone else's dream. His eyes are bright and sparkle like the sight of me is the most amazing thing he has ever seen. I know because that's the way it feels when I look at him. Awkward seconds pass feeling more like hours, and I finally speak up.

"Why? I gave you all of me and—" Dixon wipes my tears away with his thumb then sweeps it over my trembling lip.

"That's why I'm here, Hadley. They got it all wrong, it was a fuckin' ambush. That girl came out of nowhere and jumped me. If they had kept the cameras rollin' a little longer, you would've seen me push her away and sic my security team on her."

"I thought that I wasn't enough, that going on the road meant going back to your old habits."

"I may be a lot of things, Hadley, but one thing I'm not is a fuckin' liar. Sure, I used to be the guy who wanted to get high and fuck every night on the road with someone new. That hasn't happened since I laid my eyes on you. A real man doesn't do that to the woman he loves."

Why hadn't I truly seen it before? I've met the real man. Spent time with him, and God help me I've fallen in love with him, too.

"Phoenix," I whisper his name. His scent winds its way through my mind, pulling up every happy emotion and immersing me deeper in want and need. His tongue dances and duels with my own as he claims my mouth; the kisses grow more intense and passionate. There is no doubt that I am his. It's up to me now to make certain he understands that I belong to him. My worry is no longer about going too far and getting hurt, but not going far enough. I've been without a love like his long enough, and the thought of never knowing his touch again kills me inside. I'm willing to risk my heart all the way.

"Phoenix Dixon, I love you, too."

"Fuck!" I'm one lucky man. My body is exhausted from the show and flight late last night, but waking up here with Hadley makes it all worth it. Now that sweet ass vixen is beneath the covers wishing my cock a good morning. As much as I want her to keep going, I need her to stop so we can talk.

"Hey, come here." I guide her up to lay on my chest and pull the covers around us. "As much as I love that fuckin' mouth of yours on me, I need to say a few things." She props her chin up on her hands, watching me curiously. "No one has ever heard those words from me. Not ever. You are more to me than some sexual playmate. I want you to know that I do love you, Hadley. Being with me means putting up

99

with a lot of fucked up shit. It comes with the territory, and I need you to be on my side. Just because some asshole puts something on the news about me doesn't make it true. You have to trust me. It hurt, Hadley. No one has ever had the ability to hurt me like that, but you did. You think for one minute I'd be willing to give this up over some random chick?" I reach down and grab her ass to make my point.

"You were out of control. You refused to take my calls then went on a tirade of breaking the television and your phone. Did I leave anything out?" Don't get me wrong, I'm not into crazy jealous bitches by no means. In a fucked up way, I love the fact that she felt so much for me in such a short amount of time. My mama always said when the time came the right girl would just knock me on my ass. And sure as shit that's what this little spitfire has done.

"I also got into a fight with my best friend when she tried to defend you."

"Well, sounds like you have a hell of a mess to clean up. Time to start with your punishment."

She swallows hard and her eyes grow wide as I turn and pull her into me.

"You belong to me, Hadley. This. Is. All. Mine."

"Mine," Dixon growls into my ear, nibbling on my lobe. His body presses firmly against mine. He said punishment, but I'm not afraid that he would hurt me.

Sliding down my body, he grabs both of my breasts into his hands and bites the nipples. "These are mine."

I feel that tingling that starts in my spine and rests between my legs. He slips his hand down between us. My body already reacting to his words and touch. With his thumb, he tortures my clit while his pinky finger plays in my ass.

"Oh God," I moan. I reach down to hold his hand in place as my hips push harder against him. I need to come.

"No one else gets to touch these but me," he growls, "and when you're being punished, you don't get to come."

"Phoenix," I whine, and he removes his fingers from me. He stops touching me completely. He crawls out of the bed and stands at the edge. My eyes immediately go to his rock-hard cock, pointing straight at me. I swear if I didn't know any better, I'd say it growled at me, too.

He slides my legs down to the side of the bed and steps between them.

"I'm going to fuck you fast and hard. Using your body for my pleasure. Not even gonna care if you come or not. Do you know why, Hadley?" Dixon asks as he strokes his hand down his deliciously hard dick.

"Because I've been bad."

"And."

"I need to be punished."

He enters me hard; there's no slow and gentle about this. I feel the fear, anger, and frustration in each thrust. Punishing my pussy.

Several times I try to squeeze my walls around his cock to reach orgasm. He only thrusts back faster and harder in return.

Dixon is punishing me. My pussy aches. The muscles in my legs burn from being held in this position for so long. I try my hardest to catch my breath, to find some release from this wild ride I'm on. Clenching the bed sheets tighter I scream.

"Fuck. Shit. I can't take much more, Dixon."

"I don't give a fuck," he growls in that sexy tone of his. Just like that, he withdraws from me. Thinking the moment is over, I sigh breathlessly, giving my body the chance to regroup.

Wrong.

"Turn over. Put that ass up in the air for me," he commands, and I obey.

Dixon doesn't enter me right away, instead he teases. He runs the length of his hard cock up and down the crack of my ass. It's pure torture, the most wonderful kind.

Then, in one swift, hard movement his presses through my small opening. My legs shake and my body trembles uncontrollably until he's buried completely to the hilt. Dixon has me at his mercy.

"Oh fuck!" Dixon groans out as I push back against him. He comes just like he fucks. Hard and fast. He collapses on top of me and has the audacity to ask me if I learned my lesson.

"Well, if that's going to be my punishment, I may be bad again very soon," I tease. Dixon slaps my ass.

"Well what are we going to do about the other things you messed up last night?"

DIXON

I have an idea, but I'm going to need Dixon's help. "Is it too late to ask you for a favor?"

My body is sore from being used in every way by Dixon, but I love it. I invited Trish over so that we could talk. He was right, my behavior the other night was out of control.

I know that being in love with someone as famous as Phoenix Dixon is bound to bite me in the ass at least once. Yes, Dixon is one of those guys with just one look you know he always gets what he wants. I also know that means that other girls will look at him and want to chase him, but not the other way around. He's mine. I know him in a way that most don't.

DIXON

Without taking advantage of his generosity, I ask him to see if Jackson can come out. He tells me he has just the thing planned. They have another two month break before they have to get on the road.

I ask if he plans to go back to his house, but he says he has something even better in store for us. Work isn't too much of an issue since both Trish and I work remotely. We can be anywhere in the world and still plug in.

When she knocks at the door, I can't wait to let her in. I truly messed up big time with my friend and hope that she'll accept my apology.

"Thanks for coming by."

"Of course, I would. And before you say anything. I get it. Things are weird for you now. You've entered a whole new world because of Dixon."

She's right, this is a whole new world for me on so many levels. Trish and I sit and catch up on everything. I tell her about our relationship going to the next level with use of the L-word. We talk about my insecurities and how it's best to handle them moving forward in a relationship like this. And of course, I fill her in on how upset Dixon was and how he punished me for being bad.

"Regardless of what is going on with me, it wasn't right for me to take it out on you. We've been through too much together to let anything mess up our friendship."

"I'm sorry, too."

"Why are you sorry?"

"Well, I've missed you. I get that you're all into Dixon now, but I miss our friendship and hanging out."

"I'm glad to hear you say that. Dixon wants to take us somewhere special for the next two weeks."

"Wow, that's incredible, but I don't want to be the third wheel with you two."

"Who said anything about third wheel? You got along with Jackson, right?"

"Oh honey, just because things magically worked for you, doesn't mean it's in the cards for me to have the fairy tale. Jackson is about one thing—one-night stands. I could tell, and I wasn't going to make a fool out of myself thinking it could be anything more."

"So, you want more."

"You know me, Hadley, I'm screwed up. I want things, but at the end of the day I let my fear-ridden anxieties tell me that it's impossible, so I run. I'm completely comfortable with how things are. Running I'm good at. I don't know if I even have it in me to do more. It's all I know."

Grabbing her hand, I try to convince her of what could be. "Why not try to ease into it, and see if it could *be* something more?"

"That is ridiculous. He's not here, and if he was, I'd march right on up to him and give him a piece of my mind. Then I'd kiss him long and hard and then leave him hanging," Trish proclaims.

"Okay. I dare you to do just that the next time you see him. Maybe getting away will help, but we're not seriously going anywhere with you looking like this," I say, already making my way to my closet.

"Ladies, why don't you leave that up to us." The sexy voice of my man fills the air, and I turn around to see Dixon walking through my living room with Jackson at his side.

"J, how'd you like to spend the next ten days in fuckin' paradise." Jackson is my long-time friend. I don't want to see him make the mistake I had of being gone for so long that he doesn't plant roots for himself.

"She got to you fast, man, how did you know she was it for you?" The question surprises me. I never really put too much faith in the when you know you know bullshit. Somehow the timing and everything was right for me this time. This was it for me.

"With Hadley, it isn't just about the sex, although that's phenomenal. The way she looks at me reminds me of all the things I'm capable of. Dude, I started writing some new shit, and it's really good. Becoming famous so quick, it's like I haven't had a chance to breathe. It's like looking at the world through dark tinted sunglasses with a smudge on them. I took them off and suddenly everything looks clear and bright. When I saw her, in that moment everything changed."

"Dude, does your pussy hurt?" Jackson smirks.

Glaring, I punch his shoulder. "Alright. Fuck you. Go the rest of your life being a miserable single bastard."

"Dude, Trish is just inside that door, so if you like her work that shit out." We walk into the house where Hadley is waiting with Trish. Before Trish can get away, Jackson is on her heels. Grabbing her arm, he pulls her into the next bedroom.

I have no idea what's going down in there, but I hope to God he's able to work things out. Yeah, he's had women on the road, but he's more of a homebody, one woman kind of man, and he has his eyes set on Trish.

Seeing my best friend happy is important, but also having two friends who can stick together while we're out on the road is even better.

I hear them bickering in the bedroom, so I check to make sure they are alright. "Hey... hey what's going on in here?" I knock on the door before I open it.

"Nothing I can't handle," Trish grunts out, just as stubborn as can be, then brushes past me.

"Are you sure about that?" Jackson sneers and adjusts himself before heading out to join us.

I look from Jackson to Trish; her mouth is swollen and her hair is tussled. It's easy to guess what happened. Hopefully during this time away, they can get along and work their shit out.

Once we arrive at the final destination of our road trip, I have ten glorious nights to spend with my baby and there isn't anything that's going to fuck it up.

I stalk over to Hadley and wrap her in my arms

before kissing her. "You ready for a road trip to the beach. It's a day trip to get there, but believe me, it's worth it. Once we're there, it will be nothing but sun, sand, and sex."

She gives me that smile that lifts the corners of her pretty mouth and brings a glow to those cheeks.

"Grab what you need, we can get supplies along the way. I just can't wait to get you alone," I tell Hadley with a slap to that beautiful ass of hers.

Twenty minutes later the four of us are loaded up in the Suburban and ready to go.

Thirteen fucking hours in the car. We make the turn onto Gulf View Road, and I look over at the most beautiful sight in the world. Hadley. She's mine, and this is going to be a trip we'll always remember. I glance in the rearview mirror and see Jackson and Trish are passed out. I have no idea what's going to become of them, but if this fucked up guy could get someone like Hadley, then there is hope for the rest of the world.

"Wake up, baby, we're here," I say softly and run my hand through her gorgeous auburn hair.

"Mmmm." Those fucking moans she lets out make me lose my shit. I can't wait to get her to bed and get her to make them over and over again.

DIXON

Jackson and Trish wake up, and they set to unpacking the truck and getting things inside the house.

I open the gate that leads to the private beach access that belongs to the house.

"I want to go for a quick walk with you in the moonlight, Hadley." She takes my hand and walks with me as we wander aimlessly down the beach.

"The smell of the ocean and the sound of the waves as they crash against the rocks sure is a soothing sound." Hadley's sentiment matches mine. Something about this place soothes my bones, relaxing every part of me.

Hadley sinks to her knees, pulling my shorts down with her. She teases and licks against the tip of my dick. She uses her mouth and tongue to wet my dick and tease it further with delicious circles.

"If you don't stop I'm going to explode in that pretty mouth of yours." Instead of slowing, she takes me deeper, swallowing harder and using her fist to stroke my length as she sucks. Fuck she's good, I have to dig my toes into the sand to ease off the urge to come.

"Hadley, that's amazing, but I don't want to come without being inside of that sweet pussy of yours." My balls tighten, every part of me wanting to explode right there. She digs her nails into my ass cheeks pumping my hips further into her mouth.

"Fuck!" I thrust my hips into her mouth, wanting her more and more. I come hard and feel my body start to sway. Holy hell, no one has ever had the effect on me that she did. "I told you to stop. I wanted to come buried all the way inside of you." I take her hand and pull her up from her knees. She brushes off some of the sand, and I pull her into me.

"Phoenix, just so you know; you may own my body, but this cock is mine." Hadley fists me again. "Hope you don't have a problem with that." She cocks that perfectly arched eyebrow up in a way that says I'd better not have a problem with it.

"None at all."

"Good." Her smile could light up my world and that's exactly what was happening. Before I met Hadley, I was living in black and white, but now it's like I'd stepped into the Land of Oz. *Phoenix, you aren't in Kansas anymore.* "Now take me into that bedroom and rock my world."

Picking her up over my shoulder, I smack her ass as I carry her caveman style. "No way in hell I'm saying no to that, baby."

"I could have walked," she huffs as I jog up the path from the beach to our room. I know damn well she could walk, but that's not want I want. I want to show her that I love her and that she means everything in the world to me. There's just something about Hadley that made me change the way I look at life.

We get to our room, urgently stripping our clothes from our bodies, and I show Hadley just how much I want and cherish every inch of her body. She's a goddess, and she knows it. I have one more thing up my sleeve for her, but I don't want to tell her until the timing was right. So, instead, I love her until neither of us can move for the rest of the night.

A week in paradise with Phoenix is exactly what I needed, and it seems like Trish and Jackson are working their problems out, too. The only time I have seen her is when Jackson and Phoenix disappeared to go to work in the recording studio on a song that just *had* to be finished, according to Phoenix.

Laying out on the beach on an oversized towel with a damn beach umbrella blocking half my sun isn't how expected my vacation to go, but Dixon doesn't want me to get a sunburn. As if I'm a five-year-old, but I think his caveman tendencies are pretty sweet sometimes.

"So, tell me how things are going with you and Jackson."

"Girl, that man is amazing in bed. I mean, he's so damn huge that it hurts, but in a good way. He makes me orgasm at least twice before he releases, and he wants to just be with me. I'm not sure I'm okay with that, though. I like being able to do me." Trish rests

118

her head on her arms as she lays on her stomach, both of us laying out with just our bottoms on.

"Yeah, I know how that goes. You don't settle down. I think he could be the one, though, if you'd give him a shot."

"I am, but the second I think it's going to be long term, I shut down. Being with Brian did that to me. I was so set on forever with him, and then he cheated. I know you know how that feels, but I have always been worried about getting attached to anyone since then."

Before I can continue our conversation, the boys come running down to the beach, yelling about people seeing us with our tops off. Trish and I just laugh as we look over at the barbarians we've come to know as our better halves.

After my top is placed back on my tits, I sit up and watch as Phoenix and Jackson do some wake boarding and just letting loose, not worrying about keeping up the persona that is to be had with being a celebrity. As long as the man doesn't do a publicity stunt like Orlando Bloom on that canoe with his eggplant flapping around, I don't care what he does out here. I know he's been with several women, more than I cared to know, but he's mine now and I don't want anyone else getting what's mine. He. Is. Mine. Oh my god. Phoenix Dixon really is with me and I'm letting him go.

His blue eyes are alight with happiness as he laughs and looks at me, running over to cover me with his wet body, effectively cooling me off and making me hot all over again. He's my center, the person who balances me out when I'm afraid I'll never get back on my axis. I won't let him go again.

What I had with him was worth fighting for.

Sitting on the stool up on stage, with Hadley and Trish sitting on the front row, makes me smile but nervous all at the same time. This song is one Jackson and I poured over in the studio to make it just right because it was my way of letting Hadley know exactly what she's done for me. The ballad has a soulful melody and is unlike anything Dixon has given to their fans.

Running my fingers through my hair as I scope out the crowd, my eyes come to rest on Hadley. "Hey everyone! I know this is going to be something you've never heard from us before, but we hope you love it as much as we loved putting it together. This song goes out to my beautiful girlfriend, Hadley

Anders."

I love the shocked look on her face, and I smile when the realization hits her that this is the song Jackson and I spent a few hours a day in the studio writing three weeks ago. I strum the chords on my guitar as the rest of the guys join in, creating a sound unlike one we'd ever done. The words I sing express everything I have for her, how she brought me out of the havoc my life had created. I was alone and losing hope that I would find someone to help me find my center again. I'm high on loving her, and I never want to give that up.

When the song ends, the crowd erupts into a whirlwind of noise, and I know this song will be one of our biggest hits. People want the sweet, love and flowers type of shit, and I never realized it until I met the woman who made me want to give her the world. Our eyes meet in that moment, and I see the tears in hers. She's shaking her head to let me know that she's fine, and Trish is grinning like the fucking Cheshire cat at Jackson. Guess that went well, too.

"Thanks to everyone who came out tonight in

Nashville! We love you guys and we will be seeing you again!" Jackson yells into the mic before we exit the stage.

The crowd screams out our name, waiting for us to do an encore. We always do it, and it never gets old. This is just as much a part of me as Hadley is, but now I have them both. She isn't going anywhere unless it involves me and vice versa. She's who I want, and when Dixon wants something…. He gets it.

MISHA ELLIOTT & PAISLEY WALKER

Other works by Misha Elliott

Billionaire Boardroom Series:

A Day for Love

The Deal

Taming the Titan (coming May 2017)

Coleman Brother Series:

The Wrangler (coming Summer 2017)

The Lawman (coming Fall 2017)

The Desperado (coming Winter 2017)

Other works by Paisley Walker

Playing With Fire

www.ingramcontent.com/pod-product-compliance
Lightning Source LLC
Chambersburg PA
CBHW060636130626
46555CB00002B/825